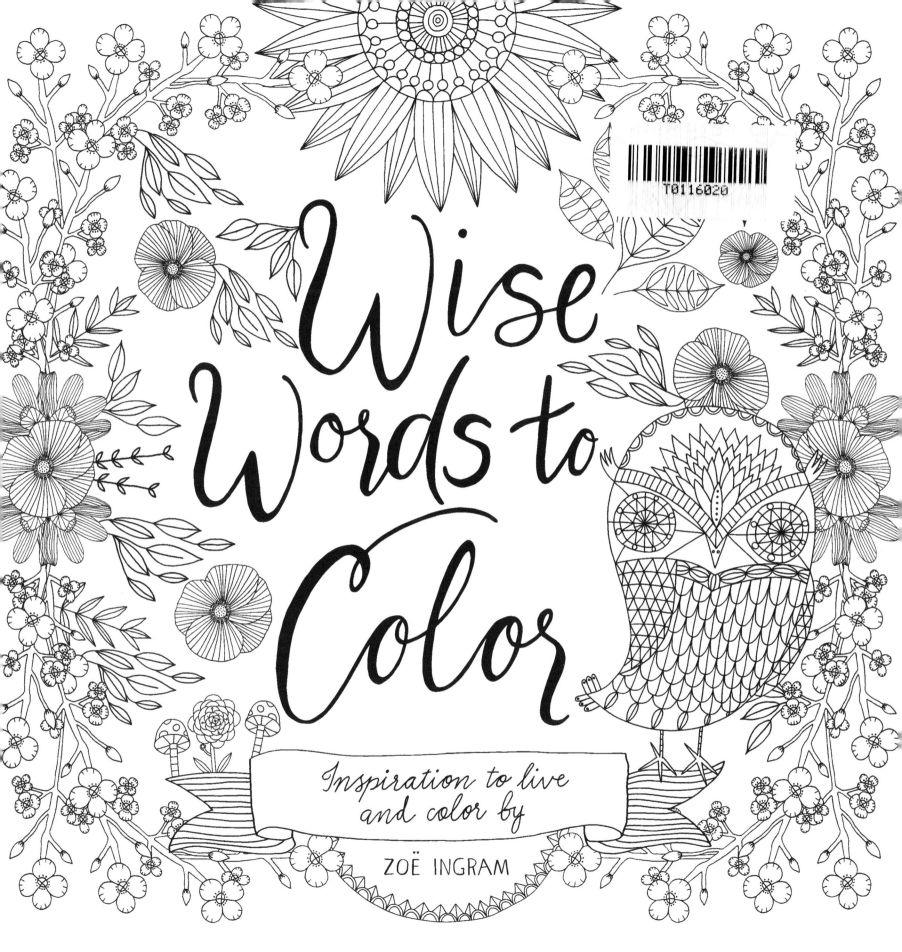

Wise Words to Color

Inspiration to live and color by

ZOË INGRAM

to Color

ZOË INGRAM

HARPER

An Imprint of HarperCollinsPublishers

For my daughters, Lexie and Poppy. You are my inspiration.
For my darling husband, Mark. Thank you for cheering me on and believing in me,
always with a cheeky grin and a wise word or two of your own.

—ZI

Wise Words to Color
By Zoë Ingram

For information address HarperCollins Children's Books,
a division of HarperCollins Publishers, 195 Broadway, New York, NY 10007.
www.harpercollinschildrens.com
ISBN 978-0-06-248192-4

The artist used a pencil, paper, brush pens, fineliner pen, and computer to create the illustrations for
this book.

Typography by Kathleen Duncan
20 21 22 23 PC/LSCW 10 9 8 7 6 5 4 3 2

First Edition

This book belongs to

_____

About My Work

Doing my job is its own best inspiration—I love art and have wanted to be an artist since I was a small child. When I'm not working on art for a client, I'm usually painting and drawing for myself. However, if I'm stuck on a project or unsure what to do, I find that picking up my knitting needles is great as a soothing meditation.

If I'm looking for visual inspiration, though, it's just outside my window! My family moved to Australia from Scotland a few years ago, and I find that the bright colors and incredible flora and fauna are great for a creative spark—you can step outside your front door and see a cockatoo or wild parrots.

For this project I found that as I was drawing the wise words that the book gets its name from, they became a mantra as I finished each piece—inspiring and teaching me as I went!

This book is a collection of all the things that inspire me most—from beautiful landscapes and bustling cities to the words of famous authors and thinkers. These are the things that spark my creativity!

I initially use a pencil for sketching out the rough outline of a piece. After that, I like to vary my process! I might use brush pens for a looser line or a wide variety of fineliner pens for a tighter line with different thicknesses. I really like to experiment and try out new techniques as I'm drawing. Finally, I scan things in and use a digital program to clean up the art—to get rid of any spare lines or smudges and make sure everything looks good.

Now, you can make these designs your own! The choice is yours—experiment with colored pencils, gel pens, or felt-tip pens. Play with colors; there are no hard and fast rules and there's room to have fun. It's your book, so be as experimental as you please. Don't color it as if there's someone looking over your shoulder! I still remember the sense of accomplishment I had as a kid when I colored in a picture really well—I hope you come away from coloring my book feeling just as inspired and ready to take on the world!

Zoë Ingram

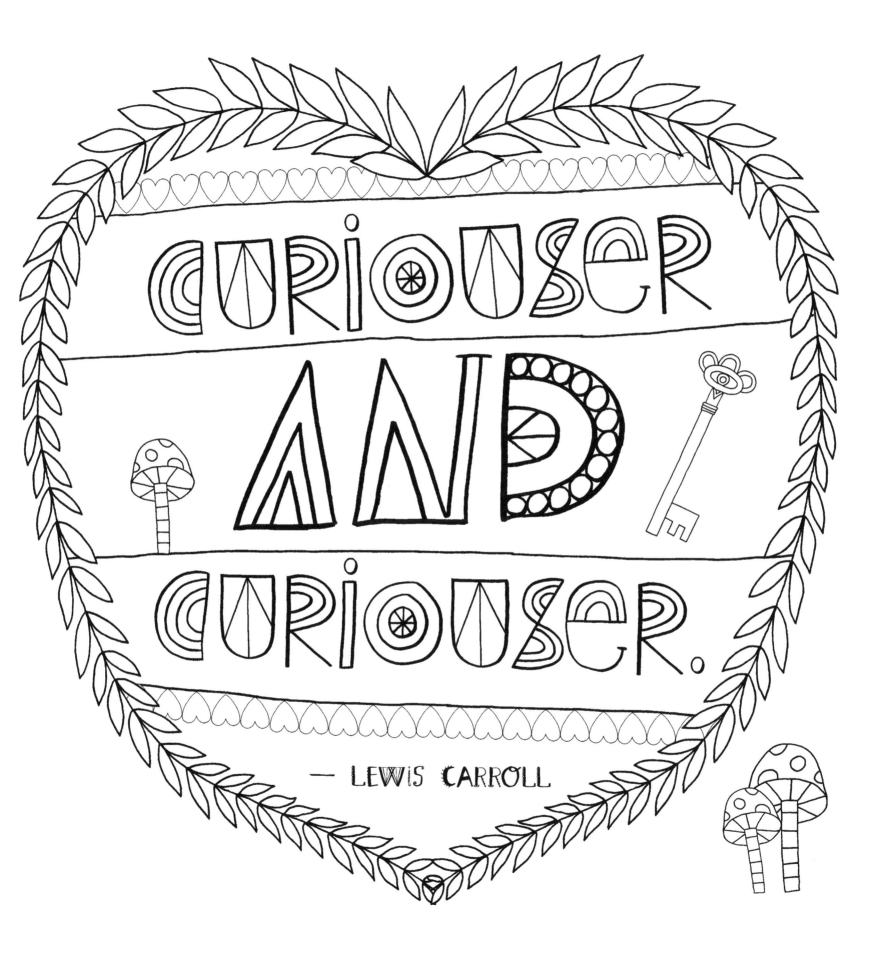

CURIOUSER AND CURIOUSER.

— LEWIS CARROLL

You can tell the character of every man when you see how he receives praise.

- Lucius Annaeus Seneca

Always do what you are AFRAID TO do.

— Ralph Waldo Emerson

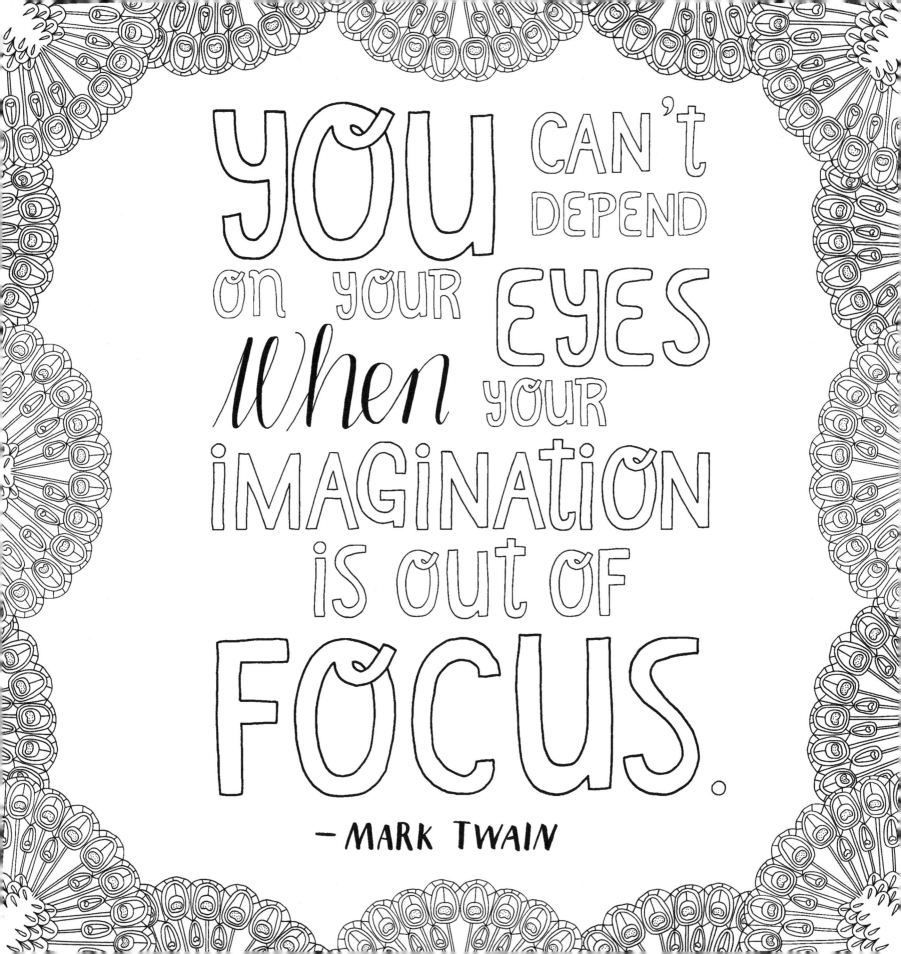

YOU CAN'T DEPEND ON YOUR EYES When YOUR IMAGINATION IS OUT OF FOCUS.

— MARK TWAIN

The best and most beautiful things in the world cannot be seen nor even touched, but just felt in the HEART.

— HELEN KELLER

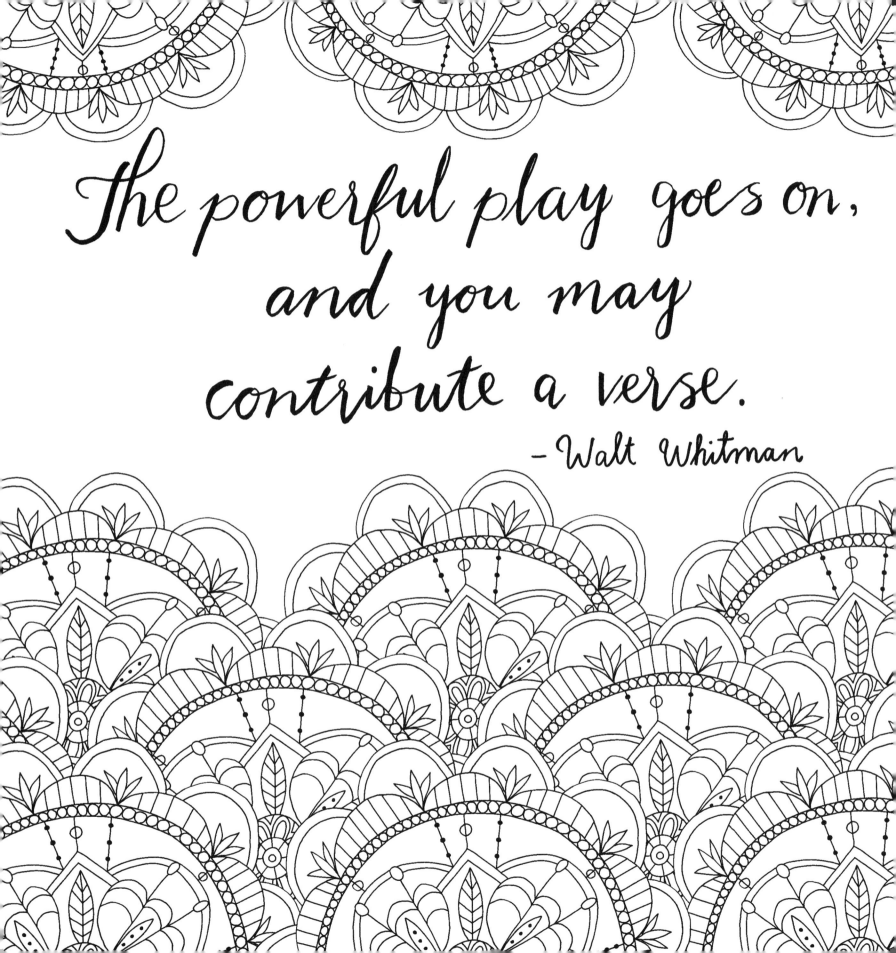

The powerful play goes on,
and you may
contribute a verse.
    – Walt Whitman

To see a WORLD IN A GRAIN OF SAND

-WILLIAM BLAKE

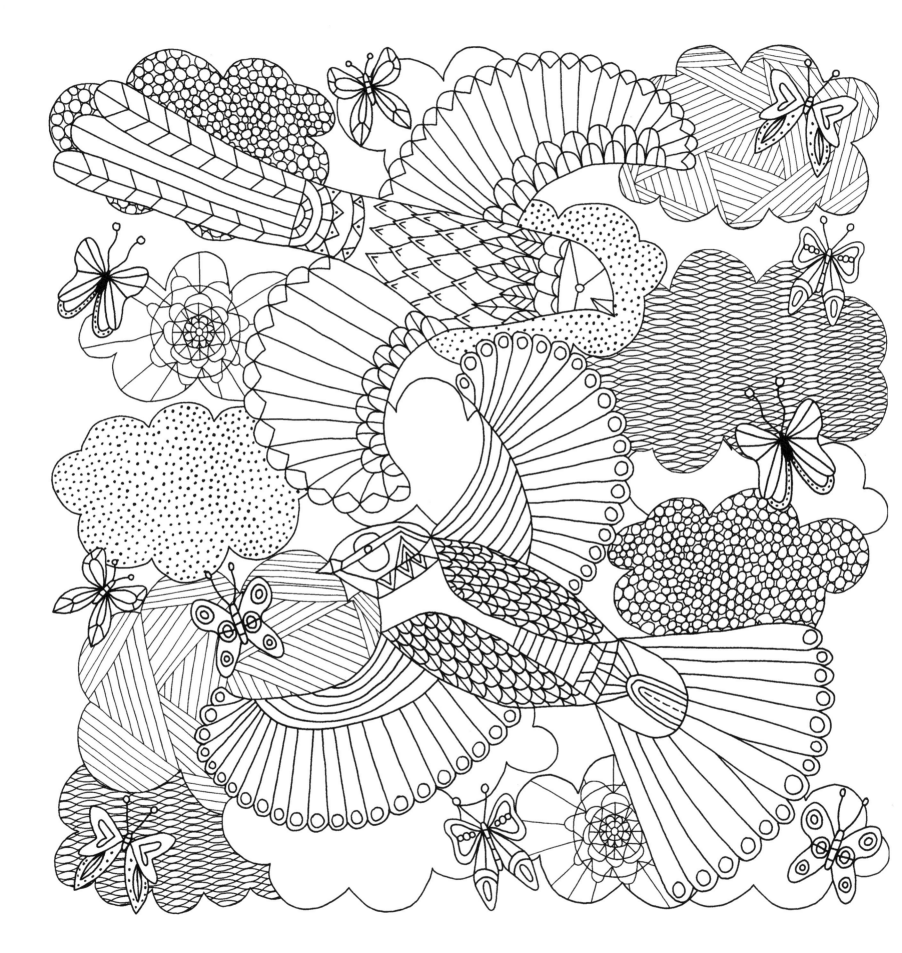

We never know how high we are
till we are called to rise;
and then, if we are true to plan,
our statures touch the skies.

— EMILY DICKINSON

we are all in the GUTTER, but some of us are LOOKING at the STARS

~ Oscar Wilde

I
invent
nothing;
I
rediscover.

– Auguste Rodin

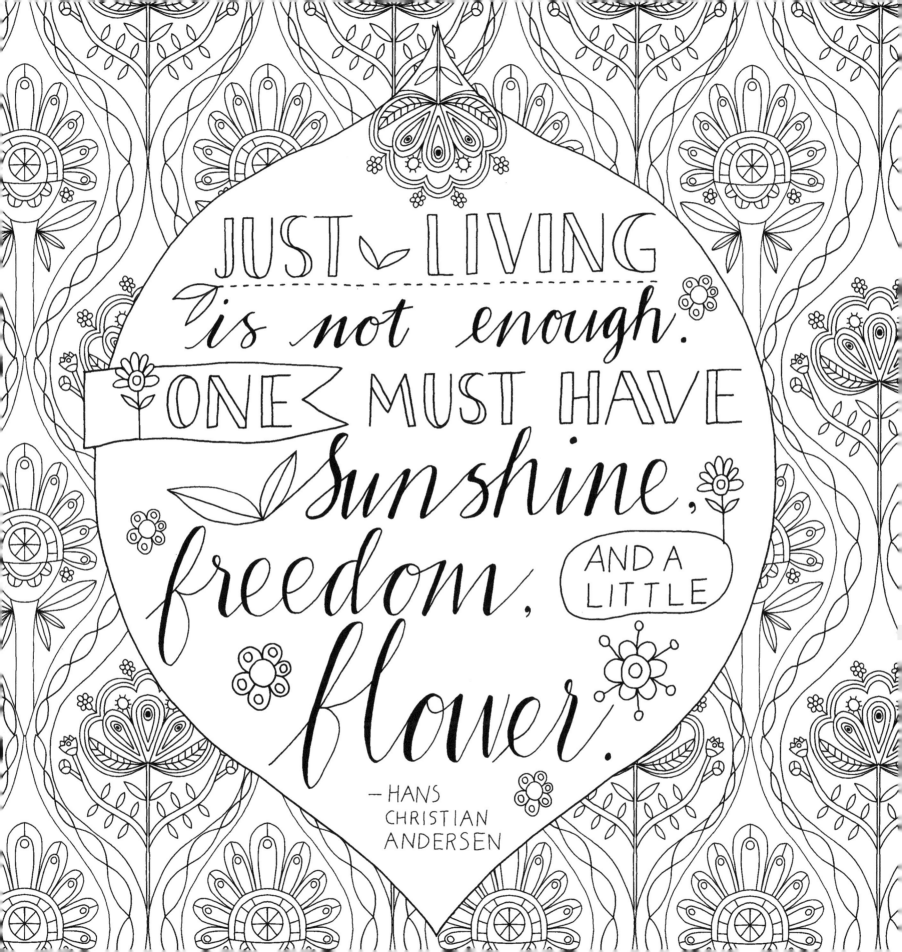

There is as much Dignity in tilling a field as in writing a poem.

— BOOKER T. WASHINGTON

LEAVE THE BEATEN TRACK AND DIVE INTO THE WOODS.

—ALEXANDER GRAHAM BELL

"If we walk far enough,"
SAID Dorothy,
"We shall sometime come to some place."

—L. FRANK BAUM

Love sought is good, but given unsought is better.

— William Shakespeare

Think in the morning,
Act in the noon,
Eat in the evening,
Sleep in the night.

—WILLIAM BLAKE

Time discovers truth.

– Lucius Annaeus Seneca

WHY,
SOMETIMES
I'VE BELIEVED
AS MANY AS SIX
IMPOSSIBLE
THINGS BEFORE
BREAKFAST.
— LEWIS CARROLL

It is difficulties that show what men are.

—EPICTETUS

MAKE INTERESTING MISTAKES, MAKE AMAZING MISTAKES, MAKE GLORIOUS & FANTASTIC MISTAKES.

— Neil Gaiman

if a tree dies, plant another in its place.

— Carl Linnaeus

THE
unexamined
LIFE
is not worth
LIVING.

—PLATO

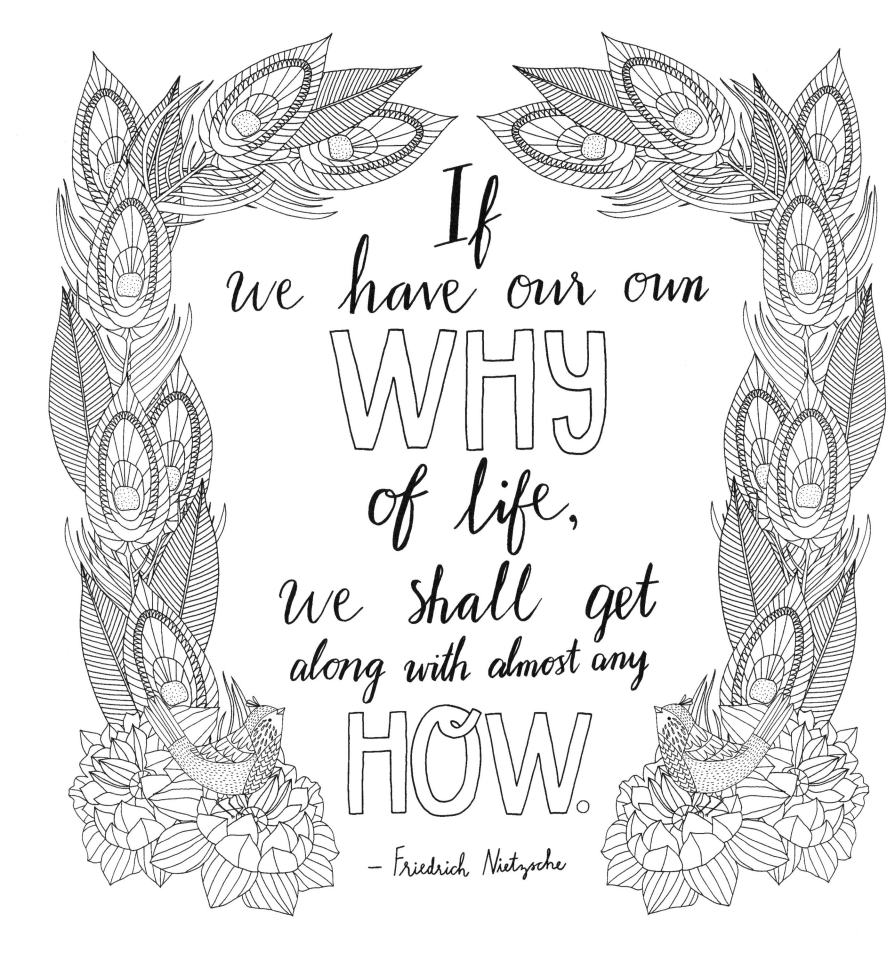

If we have our own
WHY
of life,
we shall get
along with almost any
HOW.

— Friedrich Nietzsche

Always do right.
This will gratify
some people,
and astonish
the rest.

— MARK TWAIN

I AM A PART OF ALL THAT I HAVE MET.

— ALFRED LORD TENNYSON

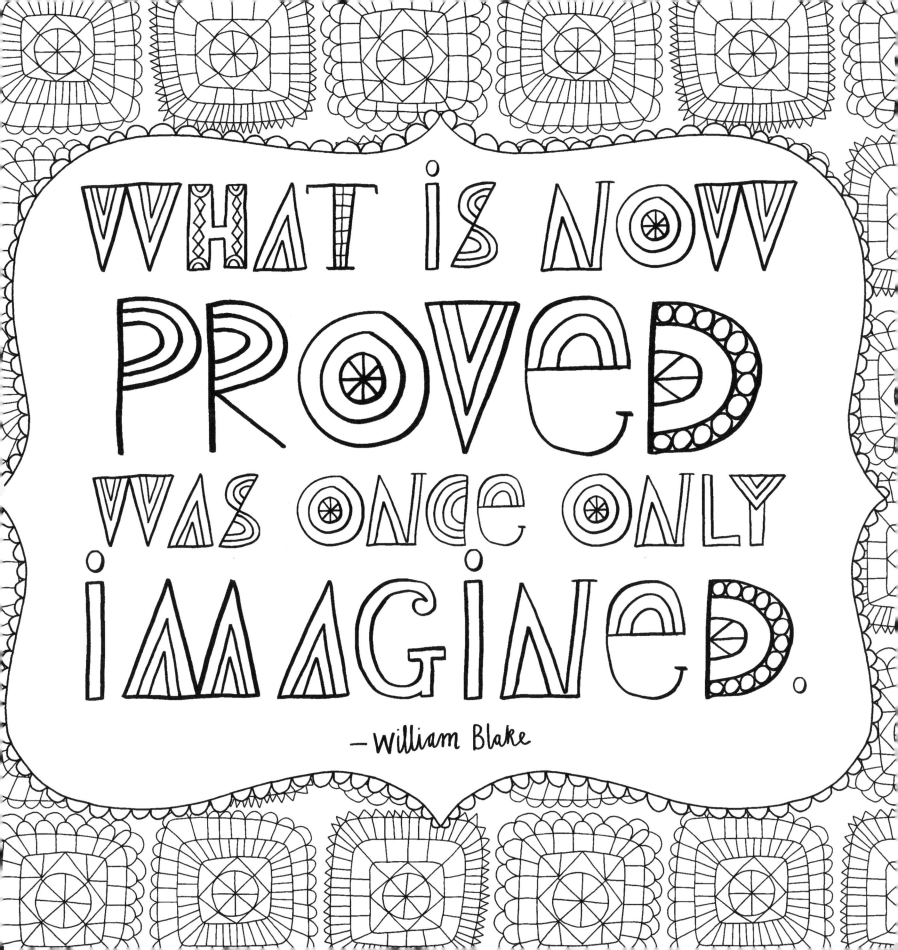

WHAT IS NOW PROVED WAS ONCE ONLY IMAGINED.

—William Blake

WE ARE SUCH STUFF AS DREAMS ARE MADE ON.

— William Shakespeare

I KNOW WHAT THINGS ARE GOOD: FRIENDSHIP AND WORK AND CONVERSATION. THESE I SHALL HAVE.

—RUPERT BROOKE

Although the world is full of SUFFERING, it is full also of the overcoming of it.

— HELEN KELLER

He who knows
other men is
discerning;
he who knows himself is
intelligent.

— LAOZI

UNFOLD YOUR OWN MYTH.

~Rumi

I HAVE PERCEIV'D THAT TO BE WITH THOSE I LIKE IS ENOUGH.

— Walt Whitman

What is a cynic?
A man who knows
the price of
everything
and the value
of nothing.

~ Oscar Wilde

Leave the world more interesting for your being here.

—NEIL GAIMAN

What must
be done
is best done
cheerfully.

— Laura Ingalls Wilder

List of Quotes

"No pessimist ever discovered the secrets of the stars."—Helen Keller

"Curiouser and curiouser."—Lewis Carroll

"You can tell the character of every man when you see how he receives praise."
—Lucius Annaeus Seneca

"Always do what you are afraid to do."—Ralph Waldo Emerson

"I have measured out my life with coffee spoons."—T. S. Eliot

"You can't depend on your eyes when your imagination is out of focus."—Mark Twain

"The best and most beautiful things in the world cannot be seen nor even touched, but just felt in the
heart."—Helen Keller

"The powerful play goes on, and you may contribute a verse."—Walt Whitman

"I like good strong words that mean something."—Louisa May Alcott

"To see a world in a grain of sand."—William Blake

"We never know how high we are / Till we are called to rise; / And then, if we are true to plan, /
Our statures touch the skies."—Emily Dickinson

"We are all in the gutter, but some of us are looking at the stars."—Oscar Wilde

"I invent nothing; I rediscover."—Auguste Rodin

"Just living is not enough. One must have sunshine, freedom,
and a little flower."—Hans Christian Andersen

"There is as much dignity in tilling a field as in writing a poem."—Booker T. Washington

"Leave the beaten track and dive into the woods."—Alexander Graham Bell

"'If we walk far enough,' said Dorothy, 'we shall sometime come to some place.'"—L. Frank Baum

"Love sought is good, but given unsought is better."—William Shakespeare

"Think in the morning, act in the noon, eat in the evening,
sleep in the night."—William Blake

"Time discovers truth."—Lucius Annaeus Seneca

"I am out with lanterns, looking for myself."—Emily Dickinson

"Why, sometimes I've believed as many as six impossible things before breakfast."—Lewis Carroll

"I am large, I contain multitudes."—Walt Whitman

"It is difficulties that show what men are."—Epictetus

"Wherever in any country the whole people feel that the happiness of all is dependent upon the happiness of the weakest, there freedom exists."—Booker T. Washington

"Optimism is the faith that leads to achievement; nothing can be done without hope."
—Hellen Keller

"Make interesting mistakes, make amazing mistakes, make glorious and fantastic mistakes."
—Neil Gaiman

"If a tree dies, plant another in its place."—Carl Linnaeus

"The unexamined life is not worth living."—Plato

"If we have our own *why* of life, we shall get along with almost any *how*."—Friedrich Nietzsche

"Always do right. This will gratify some people, and astonish the rest."—Mark Twain

"I am a part of all that I have met."—Alfred Lord Tennyson

"What is now proved was once only imagined."—William Blake

"We are such stuff as dreams are made on."—William Shakespeare

"I know what things are good: friendship and work and conversation. These I shall have."
—Rupert Brooke

"Although the world is full of suffering, it is full also of the overcoming of it. "—Helen Keller

"Travel is fatal to prejudice."—Mark Twain

"He who knows other men is discerning; he who knows himself is intelligent."—Laozi

"Unfold your own myth."—Rumi

"I have perceiv'd that to be with those I like is enough."—Walt Whitman

"What is a cynic? A man who knows the price of everything and the value of nothing."
—Oscar Wilde

"Leave the world more interesting for your being here."—Neil Gaiman

"What must be done is best done cheerfully."—Laura Ingalls Wilder

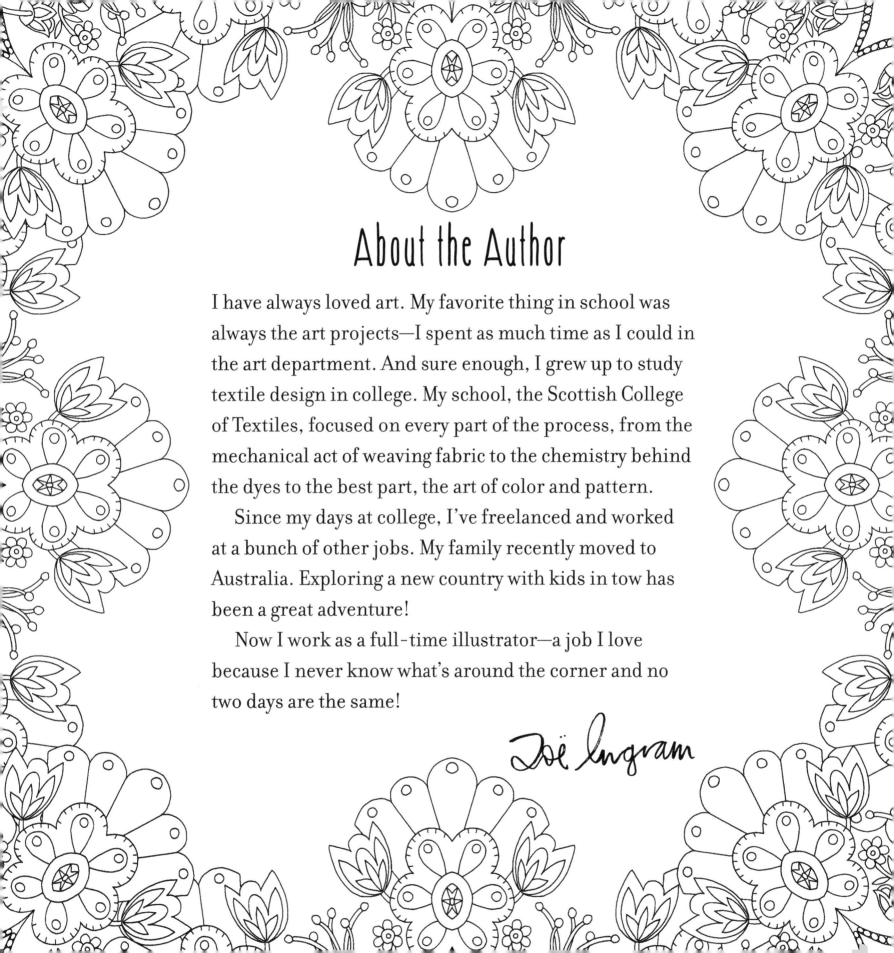

About the Author

I have always loved art. My favorite thing in school was always the art projects—I spent as much time as I could in the art department. And sure enough, I grew up to study textile design in college. My school, the Scottish College of Textiles, focused on every part of the process, from the mechanical act of weaving fabric to the chemistry behind the dyes to the best part, the art of color and pattern.

Since my days at college, I've freelanced and worked at a bunch of other jobs. My family recently moved to Australia. Exploring a new country with kids in tow has been a great adventure!

Now I work as a full-time illustrator—a job I love because I never know what's around the corner and no two days are the same!

Zoë Ingram